I Don't Ask for Much

A. D. Smith

A.D. Smith was born in Plymouth, England – a product of the 1980's.

From being a radio presenter and comedy actor in his twenties, to a father of two and divorcee during his thirties.

Now, after hitting the forty button he has a sensible job and enjoys writing stuff down that comes into his head.

This is his debut book.

For Will and Josie – I love you more than you could imagine.

However, you can read this when you're old enough!

'Give 'em plenty, one each!'

Maurice Sanger 1916 - 1998

Contents

. Platonic
. The Pub
. I'm in Love with my GP
. God Loves a Trier
. Shitting it on Streets
. Beard
. Paris
. Snip
. Phil Witchell
. Skint
. Online Dating
. Third Date Itch
. Remember This
. Terms & Conditions
. Insta
. Nothing by the Sea
. I Don't Ask for Much

Platonic

We all want something we can't have

It's the thrill of the chase

So keep your dignity old fella

She'll still think you're an ace

Is it a best mate you're after

or just a friend in kind?

You've been wishing for more

but don't know her mind

It's risk and reward

Fucks or thoughts

But this is not a game of county cricket

And the thought of losing it all

is enough to make me brick it

'Oh mate! We're fine as we are right? I'm flattered, but no...'

This is the premonition of course, I know

'I shouldn't have bothered, was I a fool to think of more?'

My natural retort, no doubt I'm sure

Let's not say anything lad

Long term it's for the best

I may lose out on a lover

But it prevents the awkwardness

Still, there will be long walks on the moor

The endless fetching of a ball

She remains the finest of her race

I told her so and said we would remain just friends

She seemed relieved, barked and wagged her tail!

The Pub

You can find me on a stool, alone with my pint

Half empty or full

It's another Monday night in the boozer

I've now become a weeknight binge loser

Alcohol and loneliness

Like brother and brother-in-law

There was once more to life than this

With no Wifi in this place

I'll give the E-dating a miss

Stop taking the piss

on myself

Yearning to kiss an analogue face

This emporium of neurotoxins

with a variety of one

Like me, has seen better, happier days

It was once a fatherly dive for the town

A place of decline subliminally spoken

It's now more renowned

as a safe haven for the superficially joyful

yet profoundly broken

Then, through the saloon door

comes regular Terry and his impressionable friend, Dave

I instantly tune into their noise and can't fathom what I'm hearing

'I'm a feminist mate!'

The old git proclaims

'I just leave it all to the women!'

The sad irony of this statement, is lost on him

Oh how I love and hate this place with a passion

and the haemorrhage it causes my wallet

Where I puke up my money

and Saturday nights without fail

the toilets are stained and smell stale

I loathe the cheap debauchery and the never-ending party anthem

Enough of this hoopla, give them bread and games

A game that plays out and spoils over Loose Women without names

So, tomorrow morning I'll phone the brewery to let them know

'It's time to sell The Lamb & Flag you know!'

But if I did, and they did too

Where the fuck would I go?

I'm in Love with My GP

Prescribing me Citalopram over Sertraline

That's why I'm in love with my GP

All my woes have been exposed

The mighty highs and potent lows

Now, there's no stopping me

'cause I'm in love with my GP

This particular Practitioner

has the reassurance I crave

Dilutes my thoughts of an early grave

Up close and personal with no further inspection

Is there something between us

apart from my twitching penis?

This infection

is infatuation

for my GP

It's the embarrassment I now die of

but I can live with the pain

These Health Care Professionals are all the same

Too professional I tell thee

Maybe it's just me?

Only I could be in love with my GP

I'll take a walk home

with the prescription I've bought

My mind will now surely be

more rational of thought

'I wonder what his wife's like?'

God Loves a Trier

She loves a trier

The scumbag of dubious morals

and a liar

Their confession 'in the office' can make a misdemeanour worthwhile

And if you believe that my friend

All is forgiven

Bless you my child

So, if you've always been a denier

Hate the morals of a scurvy

with no time for a liar

Don't worry your precious head

'Cause God too loves

God loves a trier

But false God's like her, loved too much

turn evil and exploit

I should have known

like a dog with a bone

that jaw just won't let it go

Thank the true Lord

Amen

I work for them bastard's no more

Shitting it on Streets

Panicking at checkouts

Shitting it on streets

People have the arse ache

like piles there for weeks

It can't go on forever

Something needs to give

Sod the sunny weather

we all just need to live

This cannot get much worse

Strain does take a toll

I can't see a trusted nurse

for pigment on a mole

What planet are these fuckwits from

as we show them our profanity

But the show must go on and on

despite the class disparity

Beard

My old neighbour grew a beard

And kids there thought it weird

It truly was a pretty trim

I couldn't help but to grin

At lovely Michelle whenever she neared

Paris

I once hitchhiked my way to Paris

In a rather spacious Yaris

I fell asleep in the back

Took a shit load of flak

From the driver whom I think was called Carys

Snip

My pub landlord shoots from the hip

and once told me not to go for the snip

His balls turned black

like a soot filled sack

I thanked him for the pint and the tip

Phil Witchell

I knew a lookalike of Phil Mitchell

Whom story telling was habitual

We were not friends for long

As he would get a lot wrong

And think he was writer Nick Witchell

Skint

I've got no money

Don't carry cash

This isn't funny

Where's my stash?

Penny pinch, pound punch

I'm so skint

It's toast for lunch

Working hard but living fast

An outlook short of overcast

With my empty tank

walkies to the food bank

Morsels for mere mortals

The dog gets a bone

At least they'll be dinner

when the kids get home

There's still no cash

and no one cares

I've dipped into

my stocks and shares

My monies gone

it doesn't take long

I'd sell myself

if not frowned upon

I've said it now

I'd say it twice

The breadline stinks

I'll repeat

The breadline stinks

It's not real nice

Online Dating

First class banter getting the wows

with top totty and her plucked eyebrows

It's not long before we're only pen pals

That's my online dating

Looking for…

'Only casual, nothing serious'

Sounds to me all too spurious

It's better to remain forever curious

When, you're online dating

Scroll right for the ones you like

a fair maid who looks a delight

A cold hand of 'ghosting' is totally shite

The gift from online dating

Carpet bombing all night long

Why do these messages feel so wrong?
A selfie of her wearing a tight red thong

The sleaze of online dating

Meeting half-way, let's do lunch
Buy her some flowers, just half a bunch
Keep the receipt if she's not up to much

My money pit online dating

Call me cynical
Say I'm crass
I'm looking for a lady with lower body mass
What will it take to find that lass

Online dating?

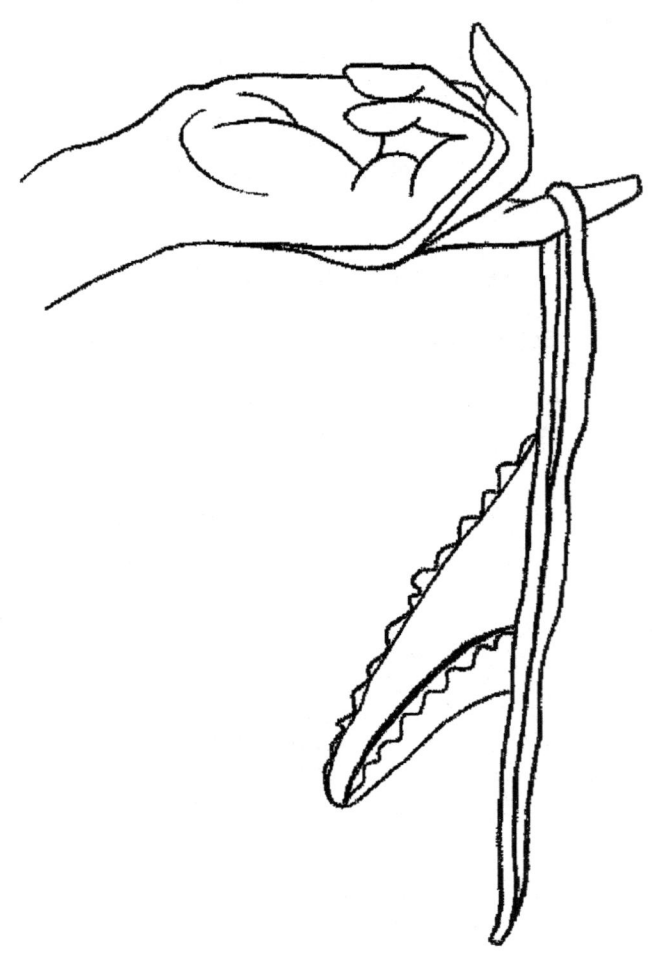

Third Date Itch

Sorry I've not text today

It's been a full-on day

I have to be honest

enjoyed your company

these past few dates

But I think it's time

to call it a day

as the stars just don't align

You're a kind, funny and

generous guy

worth knowing and

thanks for the poem

But I cannot lie

or string you along

Oh, by the way

keep the red thong!

Remember This

Remember, look up

if you're feeling down

Get off the dog and bone

Life is 'out there'

and yours to own

Whatever your vice

Smartphone and tablet

or gaming device

It's better to have lived and lost

than never to have offline lived at all

Terms & Conditions

Opt in, opt out

Tick to receive it

Tick to not

Which is it please?

I don't need the spam

Only tickets - god damn it!

For Argyle v West Ham

Insta

Instant gratification

from a pic with some geezer

Another...

by the Leaning Tower of Pisa

A pint of *Stella*

with tasty paella

Take a snap quick

with filter or two

Eat your posh grub

drink your Pilsner brew

Phew

I don't do pictorial spam

That's why I'm not on *Instagram*

Giz' a cheeky smile love

Show us where he knelt down

All the while we never see

your kids are in a meltdown

Happy families

'Living your best life!'

If only they knew the truth

you can't stand being Husband and Wife

You're off the hook

Thankfully

I don't do *Facebook*

Pedal your own agenda

Booze update from your bender

Look at all the snow!

A need-to-know basis

I really don't need to know

All the latest tit for tat

from a source that's ill informed

It can be hard to find the truth

I'm told

When reality has far from dawned

'Wanna see the Council's new Gritter?'

'Fucking hell, no!

I don't do *Twitter*'

Nothing by the Sea

The nothing town on the coast

To the naked eye it covers all bases

A glut of cafes and disabled car spaces

Ice cream parlours

Two great harbours

With Independent stores

but a *Tesco Express*

Litter on the streets

beside Herring Gull mess

When I was young this place felt cool

even with the underfunded council pool

There's no 'Oi Oi saveloy!'

with a bag of chips

Where too much salt

gives me the shits

It's not all that

but I'll be coy

We loved this town

when we were kids

I came to find joy for me

Now lost in nothing by the sea

I Don't Ask for Much

I don't ask for much

A singleton with a well-behaved canine
Best friends who arrive on time
A punishment that fits the crime

A charity tin with a note inside
Balanced individuals in a Bird Hide
Grandparents who never got ill
and died

Cinema screenings without adverts
Politicians getting their just deserts
My kids' teacher in short-fitted skirts

Estate Agents who tell the truth
Popcorn Kernels that won't break a tooth
Celebrity Love Island without a goof

Barbers not asking my holiday plans

No fifty-year-old wearing a pair of *Vans*

The M5 at Bristol without traffic jams

I don't ask for much

Premier League footballers that don't dive

The *Strictly* Results Show broadcast live

An ethical way to cheat and skive

Failure in World Cups no longer an option

One-way through the centre of Topsham

A simpler process for fixing adoption

A packet of Gnocchi with some flavour

Parking Attendents' that give a waiver

Durable batteries for my shaver

Mars bars that don't shrink in size

To understand jokes from *Morecambe & Wise*

Never again begging for a pay rise

Devon scones with cream on first

A metaphorical bubble to never burst

Tasteful artwork from Damien Hirst

I don't ask for much

Acknowledgements

Thank you for parting with some cash to have this book in your possession. If you liked it, please do me a favour and recommend to some chums. I need a new fridge!

This work was very much a mixed bag of styles, all based on a portion of fiction accompanied with a dollop of non-fiction – for added effect. I'm trusting you saw where the lines are (in real life!).

The process of writing this short book has been a long one, over the course of a couple of years. I've had a lot of shit on! However, to finally pull my finger out and get this thing published is an ambition achieved. Boom!

Heartfelt thanks must go to John A Sanger for his critique, words of wisdom and encouragement to 'just keep writing'. I did - in flurries. Also, my good friend, Pinky at The Bone Orchard for his wonderful illustrations.

I'll take all the pain and the scars of war. 'Cos I'll face the beast and fit like a matador.

Gaz Coombes © 2015

Printed in Great Britain
by Amazon